DOUGHNUTS FOR A DRAGON

Adam & Charlotte Guillain

Lee Wildish

EGMONT

A boy called George had a brilliant idea
To be like the heroes of old.
He would go off and search for a **dragon**,
To prove he was fearless and bold.

For Elisa, Nico and Joe - A&C Guillain

EGMONT
We bring stories to life

First published in Great Britain 2014 by Egmont UK Limited

This edition published in 2017

The Yellow Building, 1 Nicholas Road, London W11 4AN

www.egmont.co.uk

ISBN 978 1 4052 7054 0 (Paperback)

A CIP catalogue record for this title
is available from the British Library.

So George built a **time machine** and packed his bag
With some snacks that a hero might eat.
There were cakes, pies and buns, and a bottle of fizz,
And doughnuts - the ultimate treat.

Then George climbed aboard and he twisted a dial

So it pointed to LONG, LONG AGO.

With a WHOOSH he was off,
shooting backwards through time,

Till his time machine started to slow.

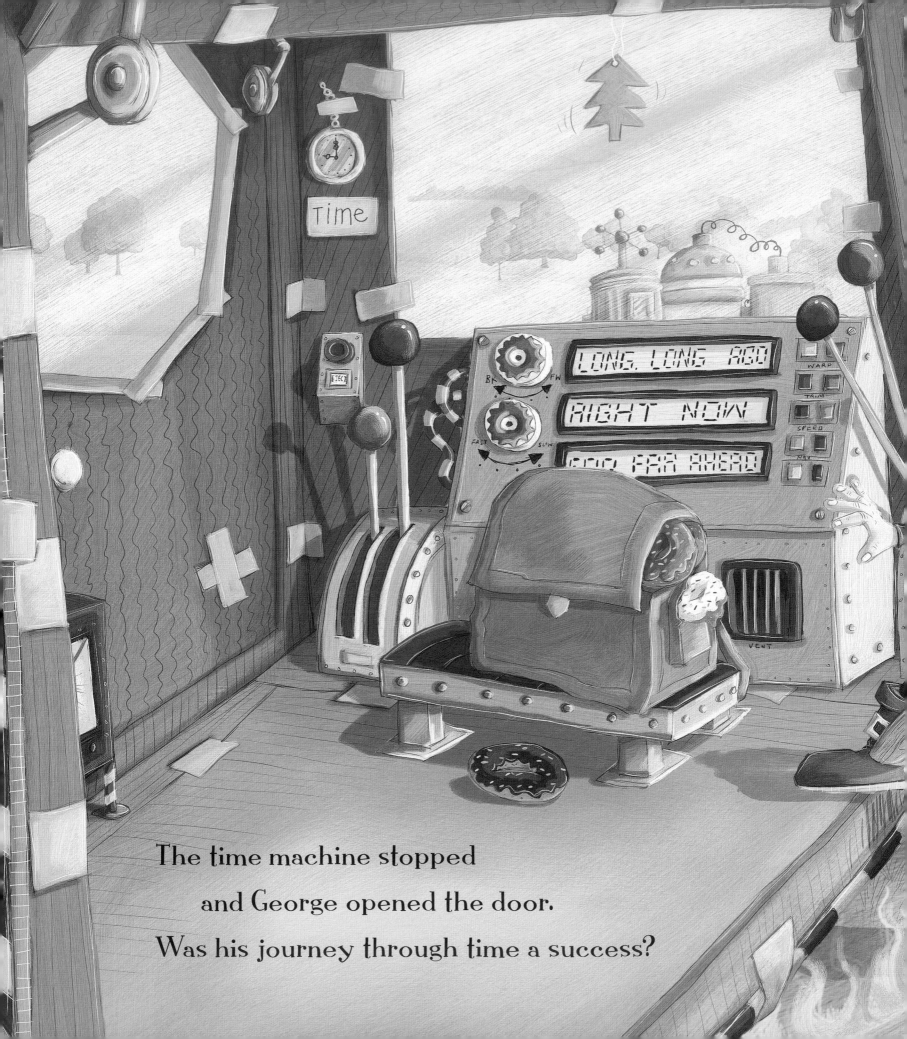

The time machine stopped
and George opened the door.
Was his journey through time a success?

He saw something lurking

behind a large bush,

Then . . .

"BOO!"
said a cheeky princess.

"I'm seeking a **dragon**!" gasped George in surprise.

"Take this map then," she said, "but beware!
There are horrible **monsters** who lurk around here,
And they'll eat you if you don't take care."

George gave her a cake to say thanks for the map

And away on his scooter he flew.

The princess looked lonely, then said to herself,

"Well then, I'll have an **adventure** too!"

George hadn't gone far when he heard a strange noise,
In the shadows he saw something sitting . . .

CLICK!
CLACK!

Was a **horrible dragon** sharpening its claws?

No - a **Witch** was just doing her **knitting!**

"Come here," said the witch
        with a sinister grin,
"I feel peckish
        and you look just right."

"Have this fruit pie instead,"
        offered George with a gulp,
"'Cause I'm seeking a dragon to fight."

"**EEEEEEK**"
shrieked the witch, and she trembled with fear.

"A dragon's a terrible brute!
It can breathe **deadly fire**
that will roast you for sure.
You'd better go home - off you scoot!"

Lake Deep

Dark Wood

Pointy Mountains

"I'm not scared," said George, and he rode further on,

Till he saw puffs of smoke up ahead.

Was a **fire-breathing dragon** lying in wait?

No - an ogre was toasting some bread!

"Yum!" said the ogre,

lifting George up,

"I'll have you for dinner tonight."

"Don't eat me!" cried George,

"Have these iced buns instead!

Cause I'm seeking a dragon to fight."

FIRE STARTER

"EEEEEEP!"

yelped the ogre in horror and fear,

"A dragon is scary and wild!
It has many sharp claws and such **jaggedy teeth**,
You should run away home, crazy child!"

The ogre ran off with a terrified howl,

And George carried on up the track.

He was starting to think he had made a mistake,

But was it too late to turn back?

Then he stopped as a shadow fell over the path,
From the branches above came a **creak**.

Was a **hideous dragon** about to attack?
Then George heard a **bone-chilling** . . .

The fierce little dragon then narrowed its eyes.

It breathed out **fiery flames** in a flash.

George reached into his bag for his bottle of fizz . . .

And he put out the fire with a **SPLASH!**

Then George pulled out a doughnut
and threw it up high,
The dragon looked up
and it froze.

It leapt off the ground and
then squeaked in surprise,
As the doughnut fell . . .

...**plop** on its nose!

The dragon looked up
and it burst into tears.
"Please stop laughing," it managed to say.
"I'm ever so lonely and never make friends –
No one sees that I just want to **play**."

Then all of a sudden the princess leapt out.

"You poor little dragon," she said,

"I want someone to play with, will you be my pet?"
Delighted, it nodded its head.

They feasted on doughnuts until the sun set,
And the dragon breathed flames hot and bright.

Then George and the princess did daredevil stunts,
And the new friends played all through the night.